CLASSIC RIDES

CLASSIC Chevelles

BY CLAIRE ROMAINE

INVESTIGATE!

Enslow PUBLISHING

Please visit our website, www.enslow.com. For a free color catalog of all our high-quality books, call toll free 1-800-398-2504 or fax 1-877-980-4454.

Library of Congress Cataloging-in-Publication Data

Names: Romaine, Claire, author.
Title: Classic Chevelles / Claire Romaine.
Description: New York : Enlow Publishing, [2021] | Series: Classic rides | Includes bibliographical references and index.
Identifiers: LCCN 2019050662 | ISBN 9781978517974 (library binding) | ISBN 9781978517950 (paperback) | ISBN 9781978517967 (6 Pack) | ISBN 9781978517981 (ebook)
Subjects: LCSH: Chevelle automobile—History—Juvenile literature.
Classification: LCC TL215.C48 R66 2021 | DDC 629.222/2—dc23
LC record available at https://lccn.loc.gov/2019050662

Published in 2021 by
Enslow Publishing
101 West 23rd Street, Suite #240
New York, NY 10011

Designer: Katelyn E. Reynolds
Editor: Therese Shea

Photo credits: Cover, p. 1 (left Chevelle) krishnaobhasa/Shutterstock.com; cover, pp. 1 (middle Chevelle), 7 (main), 11 (main) Kevin M. McCarthy/Shutterstock.com; cover, p. 1 (right Chevelle) betto rodrigues/Shutterstock.com; cover, pp. 1–32 (series chrome font) Mott Jordan/Shutterstock.com; cover, pp. 1–32 (series background) Sylvie Bouchard/Shutterstock.com; p. 4 Labrynthe/Shutterstock.com; p. 5 Art Konovalov/Shutterstock.com; pp. 7 (inset), 14, 24 Barry Blackburn/Shutterstock.com; p. 8 tomeng/iStock Unreleased/Getty Images; p. 9 Greg Gjerdingen (https://www.flickr.com/people/52900873@N07) from Willmar, USA/OceanAtoll/Wikipedia.com; p. 11 (inset) John Lloyd (https://www.flickr.com/people/32109282@N00) from Concrete, Washington, United States/Artix Kreiger/Wikipedia.org; pp. 12, 13 Sergey Kohl/Shutterstock.com; p. 15 photo-denver/Shutterstock.com; p. 17 (main) Parilov/Shutterstock.com; p. 17 (inset) Al Paloczy/The Enthusiast Network via Getty Images/Getty Images; p. 18 Steven Kelly/The Enthusiast Network via Getty Images/Getty Images; p. 19 Car Culture ® Collection/Getty Images Plus; pp. 21, 25 Tony Savino/Shutterstock.com; p. 22 Stefan Malloch/Shutterstock.com; p. 23 Sundry Photography/Shutterstock.com; p. 29 Andrew Harrer/Bloomberg via Getty Images.

Portions of this work were originally authored by Michael Portman and published as *Chevelles.* All new material this edition authored by Claire Romaine.

Printed in the United States of America

CPSIA compliance information: Batch #BS20ENS: For further information contact Enslow Publishing, New York, New York, at 1-800-398-2504.

Contents

WORDS IN THE GLOSSARY APPEAR IN **BOLD** TYPE THE FIRST TIME THEY ARE USED IN THE TEXT.

MUSCLE-CAR Nation

Beginning in the 1950s, many Americans fell in love with muscle cars. These high-powered, high-speed vehicles ruled the roads. At first, car fans created their own "hot rods." They put large, powerful engines in cars they bought and sometimes even raced each other to test their altered vehicles.

GET THE FACTS!

Chevrolet, sometimes shortened to Chevy, is one division of the GM (General Motors) car company. Other manufacturers under GM today include Buick, GMC, and Cadillac. GM was founded in 1908, and Chevrolet became a part of it in 1918.

Carmakers noticed this craze and decided to give the public what they wanted, right out of the factory. Chevrolet was one of the most successful muscle-car manufacturers of the 1960s and 1970s, and Chevelles were some of the most muscular of their fleet.

TODAY, CHEVELLES ARE CONSIDERED CLASSIC CARS AND NOT JUST BECAUSE THEY WERE PRODUCED YEARS AGO. THEY'RE ADMIRED FOR THEIR VALUE, QUALITY, AND APPEARANCE.

THE V-8 Engine

Chevrolet introduced its **V-8** engine in 1955. This fast, lightweight, and easily maintained engine was extremely popular with hot-rodders and street racers. It meant regular people could have a high-performance vehicle. It became the most successful engine in the history of NASCAR (National Association for Stock Car Auto Racing).

GET THE FACTS!

The powerful 409 was the subject of the hit Beach Boys song "409." This song helped make Chevy's big-block engine even more popular. However, the Beach Boys later admitted they didn't know much about cars or engines!

CHEVROLET PRODUCED 491,000 IMPALAS FOR 1961. ONLY 453 HAD THE SUPER SPORT PACKAGE, AND JUST 142 HAD THE 409 ENGINE. CHEVY IMPALAS WERE KNOWN FOR THEIR SPECIAL REAR STYLING.

As popular as these engines were, it was the large V-8 called the big block that made Chevy muscle cars the stuff of legend. In 1961, the Chevrolet Impala Super Sport became the first car powered by Chevy's V-8 big-block engine called the 409.

409 V-8 ENGINE

THE SUPER Sport

INTERIOR OF A CLASSIC IMPALA SS

The full-size Chevrolet Impala was introduced in 1958 and restyled in 1961. It became the first Chevy offered with a Super Sport (SS) package. This included improvements to the car inside and outside, as well as special trim, or decorations and details. Customers could choose their engine, including the 409. *Motor Trend* magazine wrote about the 1961 Impala SS with a 409 engine: "The SS will shoot away from practically anything else on the road."

GET THE FACTS!

The 1964 Pontiac Tempest GTO set the standard for muscle cars of the mid-1960s. It appeared to be just an ordinary car, but under the hood was a powerful engine. Most muscle cars followed the same pattern but took on their own look.

By the mid-1960s, however, full-size cars were falling out of favor. Midsize muscle cars were taking over.

THE 1964 PONTIAC GTO KICKED OFF THE MUSCLE-CAR CRAZE AMONG CAR MANUFACTURERS. PONTIAC, LIKE CHEVY, WAS A DIVISION OF THE GM CAR COMPANY.

INTRODUCING THE Chevelle

To answer the public's demand for a midsize muscle car, Chevrolet offered the Chevelle in 1964. It was shorter and narrower than the Impala, but it offered nearly as much room inside. The Chevelle came in a variety of styles: **coupes**, two-door and four-door **station wagons**, and four-door **sedans**.

GET THE FACTS!

Chevrolet created the Chevelle to compete against midsize cars such as the Ford Fairlane. Most car companies recognized the high demand for midsize cars and quickly created their own models. Chevrolet was one of the last companies to issue a midsize car.

Customers hoping the Chevelle would be a muscle car were disappointed at first. The Super Sport package was offered as an addition to the Chevelle's top **trim level**, the Malibu. However, even this model lacked high-**horsepower** engines. Chevy was listening to these concerns, however.

THE 1964 CHEVELLE WAS OFFERED IN THREE MODELS: THE 300, THE MALIBU, AND THE MALIBU SUPER SPORT.

GAINING Muscle

While other muscle-car manufacturers were using big-block engines, Chevelles had small-block V-8s. There was one exception. Offered midway through the 1965 model year, the limited-edition Chevelle Malibu SS Z-16 sported Chevy's new 396 big-block engine. This car could reach 1/4 mile (402 m) in about 14 seconds at a speed of around 100 miles (161 km) per hour.

GET THE FACTS!

In Southern California, cars were the center of attention in many crowds. American car companies, including Chevrolet, took advantage of that when naming their cars. Two of the Chevelle's trim levels, the Malibu and the Laguna, were named after California cities.

The 396 was the engine that replaced the famous 409. It was **designed** for Chevrolet's top-of-the-line sports car, the Corvette. Only 201 Chevelle Malibu SS **hardtops** and **convertibles** received the Z-16 package.

THE 1965 CHEVELLE MALIBU SS WAS THE TURNING POINT FOR THE CHEVELLE'S FUTURE AS A MUSCLE CAR.

THE SS 396

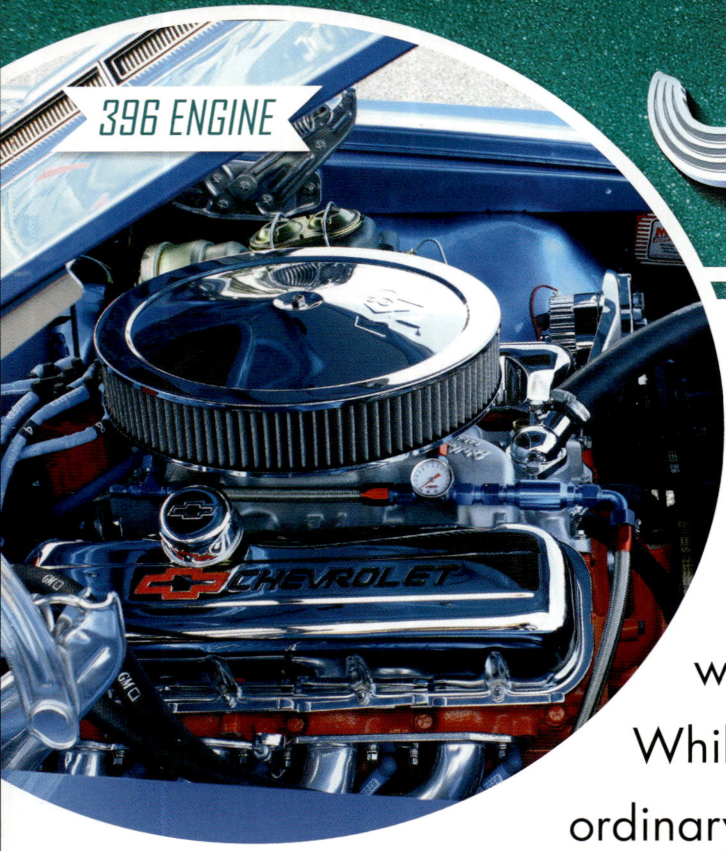

396 ENGINE

In 1966, the Super Sport became its own model rather than an option, or choice, package for the Chevelle. It was called the Chevelle SS 396. While customers could still choose an ordinary Chevelle from other trim levels, the Super Sport line featured true muscle cars.

CHEVY MADE 72,272 CHEVELLE SS 396 VEHICLES FOR THE 1966 MODEL YEAR.

Every Chevelle SS came with a 396 engine. At first, the engines in the 1966 SS 396 weren't as powerful as the one used in the Z-16. Then, Chevrolet offered a 396 engine called the L78. The L78 pumped out a whopping 375 horsepower!

GET THE FACTS!

The 1966 Chevelle SS 396 had a base price of $2,776. That's almost $22,000 in today's money. The average price of a new car in recent years is about $37,000. That means the 1966 Chevelle SS 396 was affordable too!

CHANGING THE Chevelle

While the 1966 Chevelle SS 396 had muscle-car power, it needed improvements for safer road performance. In 1967, Chevrolet made those improvements. Better tires gave the car a firmer grip on the roadway. Drivers felt more secure when changing direction. In addition, new front brakes reduced the Chevelle's stopping distance.

GET THE FACTS!

From 1964 until 1977, the Chevrolet El Camino coupe was based on the Chevelle platform, the name for Chevelle's design, size, and power. The El Camino was called a utility vehicle. It was part car, part pickup truck!

SIDE BADGE

ONE REASON FOR THE 1967 CHEVELLE'S REDUCED HORSEPOWER WAS THAT GM WANTED TO KEEP HIGH-HORSEPOWER ENGINES FOR ITS LINE OF CHEVY CORVETTES!

But, instead of maintaining or increasing the horsepower of the Chevelle SS 396's engines, Chevrolet decreased it. It was a strange direction to take for a muscle car in 1967, but the loss of power didn't really hurt sales figures.

In 1968, Chevy gave its Chevelles a new look. The wheelbase, or the distance between the centers of the front and rear wheels, was shortened by 3 inches (7.6 cm). Past Chevelles had been full of sharp lines and angles. The new design was curvier. Its **grille** had a new look too.

GET THE FACTS!

The full-size 1968 Chevy Impala had a wheelbase of 119 inches (302 cm), and the compact 1968 Chevy Corvair had a wheelbase of 108 inches (274 cm). The 1968 Chevelle SS 396 was in the middle with a wheelbase of 112 inches (284 cm). That's why it was called a midsize car.

The Chevelle SS 396 had four engine choices, including the 375-horsepower 396 L78 last seen in 1966 models. But big-block engines were heavy, so cars that carried them were harder to handle. The 1968 Chevelle SS 396 was no exception.

THE 1968 CHEVELLE SS 396 GOT SOME POWER BACK. MODELS WITH THE L78 ENGINE BOASTED 375 HORSEPOWER.

RECORD Breaker

In 1969, Chevrolet turned the SS 396 into a special package available on Chevelle coupes and convertibles. Even though it wasn't a separate trim level, the Chevelle SS 396 was as powerful as ever. Its nose curved down, reminding fans of a race car. Chevrolet decorated it inside and out with eye-catching "SS 396" **emblems**. Chevelles also received newly designed taillights.

GET THE FACTS!

The Chevelle SS moved fast on the road and at the dealership. In 1968, Chevrolet made 57,600 Chevelle SS 396s. It produced 28,707 more 1969 models. Chevrolet built almost 296,000 SS 396s and SS 454s from 1968 to 1972.

A CAR AND DRIVER MAGAZINE REVIEWER CALLED THE 1969 CHEVELLE SS 396 L78 EDITION THE "BADDEST MOTOR IN TOWN!"

The 1969 Chevelle SS 396 sold a record 86,307 models, with more than 9,000 carrying the powerful L78 engine. The muscle-car age was about to reach its peak.

THE SS 454

TAILLIGHTS IN BUMPER

By 1970, many car companies were producing muscle cars. It wasn't easy to stand out from the crowd. Bright colors, racing stripes, and **spoilers** could make a car look fast, but they didn't make a difference where it really counted—under the hood.

GET THE FACTS!

For 1970, Chevrolet redesigned the Chevelle again. It had the same basic shape as the 1968 and 1969 models, but it sported a simpler, cleaner look. Chevelle SS models could be ordered with two large racing stripes on the hood.

Chevrolet didn't need tricks for its 1970 Chevelle SS, although it did have new styling. It relied on horsepower. GM finally allowed Chevy cars other than Corvettes to increase their horsepower. The 1970 Chevelle SS 454 was one of the cars to benefit from this power boost.

NEW LAWS CALLED FOR THE TAILLIGHTS OF THE 1970 CHEVELLE SS TO BE PLACED IN THE BUMPER.

The Chevelle SS 454 was Chevrolet's contender in the muscle-car competition of the early 1970s. The SS 454 package offered customers a choice of engines—the LS5 and the LS6. The LS5 produced 360 horsepower. The LS6 produced 450 horsepower!

The Chevelle SS 454 was a heavy car. However, even at nearly 3,800 pounds (1,725 kg), it was fast. Improvements gave it excellent handling, though. It took just 6.1 seconds to hit 60 miles (97 km) per hour and 13.7 seconds to finish 1/4 mile (402 m).

GET THE FACTS!

Customers could choose Chevy's cowl-induction system. This system placed a flap near the base of the windshield that opened when the driver pressed the gas pedal. The increased airflow allowed the engine to "breathe" and increased its performance.

MEASUREMENTS OF THE 1970 CHEVELLE SS 454

LENGTH: 197.2 INCHES (501 CM)

HEIGHT: 52.6 INCHES (133 CM)

WEIGHT: 3,759 POUNDS (1,705 KG)

LS6 ENGINE POWER: 450 HORSEPOWER

FUEL CAPACITY: 20 GALLONS (76 L)

WHEELBASE: 112 INCHES (284 CM)

MANY ENGINES ARE NAMED FOR THEIR SIZE. THE 454, FOR EXAMPLE, IS 454 CUBIC INCHES (7,440 CC). THE LS5 AND LS6 ARE DIFFERENT TYPES OF THIS ENGINE.

THE END of the Road

The SS 454 was not only the most powerful Chevelle, it was among the most powerful muscle cars. It hit the fastest times a Chevelle would ever record. The muscle-car age came to an end in the 1970s. Rising fuel costs caused a demand for more **fuel-efficient** cars. New laws required that cars be safer and produce less air pollution. Design changes meant heavier cars with less power. The Super Sport name came to be more about style than power.

Chevrolet made the Chevelle until 1977. In 1978, the Chevy Malibu replaced it.

GET THE FACTS!

In 1972, Chevrolet issued a Chevelle SS called the Heavy Chevy. The Heavy Chevy looked like a muscle car but lacked some features of a standard Chevelle SS. The powerful 454 LS6 engine wasn't a choice for the Heavy Chevy.

CHEVELLE PRODUCTION NUMBERS

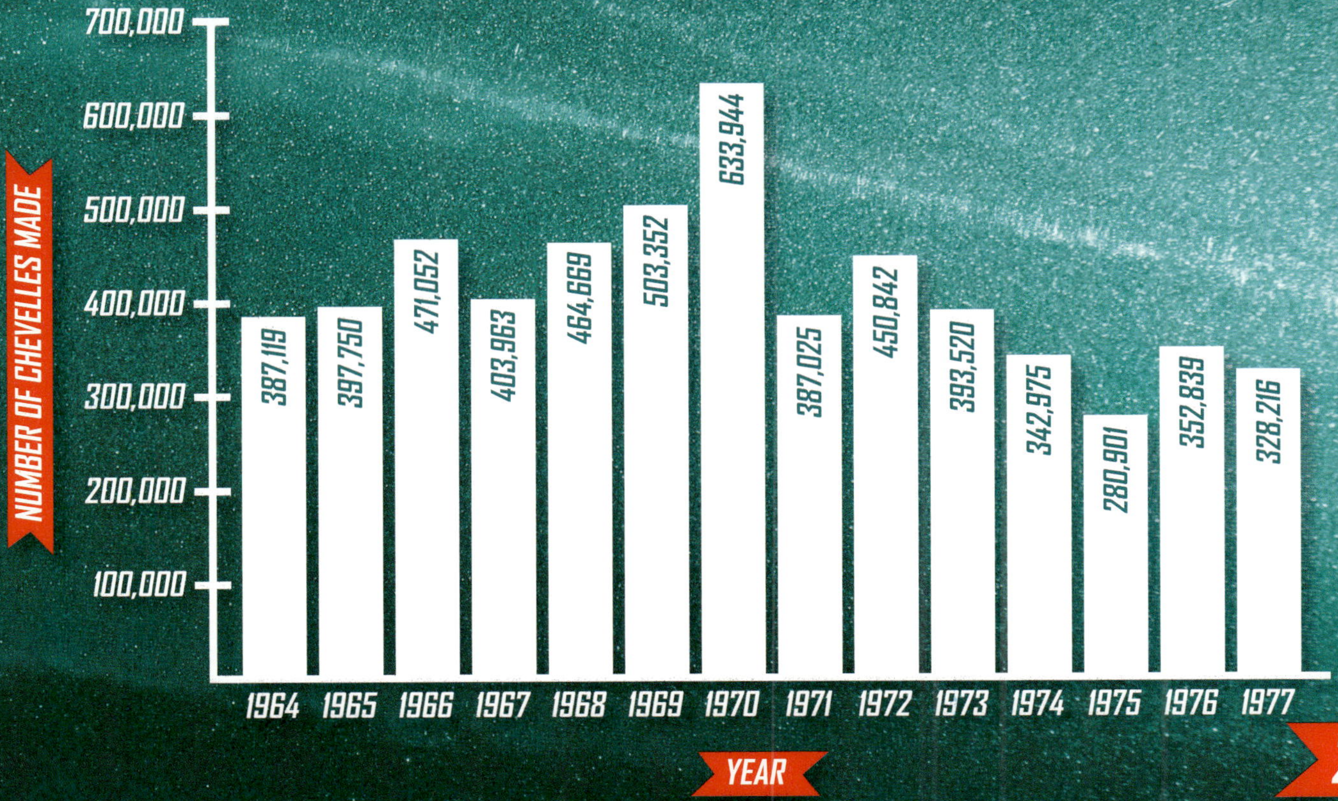

A NEW *Chevelle?*

New Chevelles may not be available, but older ones are. In fact, Chevelles have become a collector's car. In 2013, a 1970 Chevrolet Chevelle SS 454 LS6 sold for over $1 million!

For years, Chevelle fans have hoped Chevy would bring back their beloved muscle car. Will Chevy listen to its fans and produce a modern muscle-car king? Until then, car buffs will continue to appreciate the beauty of these vehicles at classic car shows and other events at which people can show off their Chevy Chevelles.

GET THE FACTS!

The 1976 Chevelle Laguna S-3 was king of the NASCAR track in the mid-1970s. Driver Cale Yarborough, winner of three Winston Cup championships in a row, drove to victory many times in a Laguna S-3. NASCAR banned the car in 1977.

SOME PEOPLE BELIEVED THIS 2012 CHEVY CONCEPT CAR, CALLED THE CODE 130R, WOULD BECOME A NEW VERSION OF THE CHEVELLE. FANS CAN ONLY HOPE!

Glossary

convertible A car with a roof that can be lowered or removed.

coupe A two-door car with one section for the seat and another for storage space.

design To create the plan or form of something.

emblem A sign that represents an object, idea, group, or quality.

fuel-efficient The quality of being able to operate using little fuel, or without waste.

grille A metal screen on the front of a car that allows cool air into the engine.

hardtop A two-door or four-door car without a center door post.

horsepower A unit used to measure the power of an engine.

sedan A car with front and back seats, two or four doors, an enclosed body, and a permanent top.

spoiler A wing-shaped device attached to the back of a car to improve airflow and stability.

station wagon A car with an extended area behind the rear seats.

trim level The features and decorations included in a car's options package.

V-8 A kind of engine that has two sets of four chambers at an angle to each other.

FOR MORE INFORMATION

BOOKS

Harrison, Paul. *Racing Supercars*. Mankato, MN: Arcturus Publishing, 2015.

Mason, Paul. *American Supercars: Dodge, Chevrolet, Ford*. New York, NY: PowerKids Press, 2019.

Worms, Penny. *Sports Cars*. Mankato, MN: Smart Apple Media, 2016.

WEBSITES

Classic Muscle Cars
musclecars.howstuffworks.com/classic-muscle-cars/
Check out this great muscle-car resource.

Race Cars
www.dkfindout.com/us/transportation/history-cars/race-cars/
Read about race cars and take a quiz.

Index

CLASSIC RIDES

Titles in this Series

- CLASSIC CAMAROS
- CLASSIC CHARGERS
- CLASSIC CHEVELLES
- CLASSIC CORVETTES
- CLASSIC GTOS
- CLASSIC PORSCHES

Enslow PUBLISHING

ISBN: 9781978517950
6-pack ISBN: 9781978517967
9 781978 517950

I LIKE SHIH TZU!

Linda Bozzo

DISCOVER DOGS WITH THE AMERICAN CANINE ASSOCIATION